Sappy Stuff

For Megan, Sebastian, Natalie, Jacob & Micah.
I love you each more than air!
Lincoln: Love is believing in someone even when they have trouble believing in themselves and obviously YOU know this.
Dololah: You totally rock at this friendship thing!
And to Dominic, thank you for making Kyle come to life!

I'd Rather Eat Mud

by Lorenza Krautkraemer

My mom is a good cook. She cooks all the time. Her meatball spaghetti is a favorite of mine.

She cooks all
these foods
that I really
do love
but when she
cooks broccoli,

I'd rather eat MUD!!

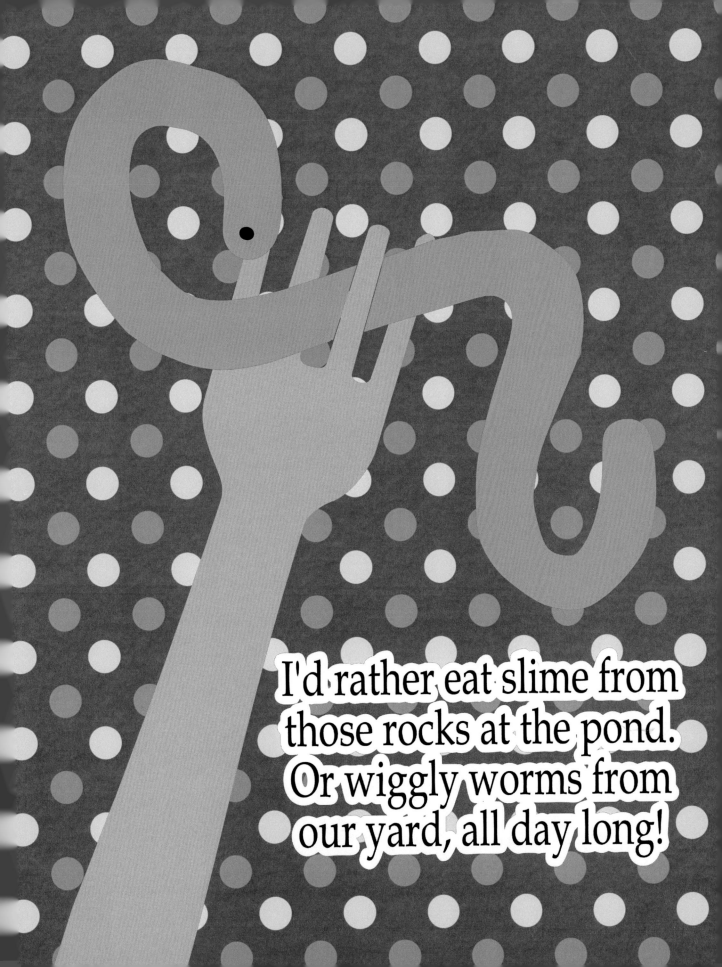

I'd rather eat slime from those rocks at the pond. Or wiggly worms from our yard, all day long!

I'd rather eat snails or a
dozen raw eggs!
A million small spiders
with long, skinny legs!

Mom knows that I can't stand that stuff
Just looking at broccoli is hard enough.
But still at dinner this very night,
before I could put up a fight,

I'd rather eat ice cubes made out of mustard, or maybe some crispy gravel with custard! You make lots of food that I really do love but when you cook broccoli

I'd rather eat MUD!

Mom just looked at me,
calm as could be.

You would rather eat mud
than eat broccoli?

I crossed my arms, my
chin held high.

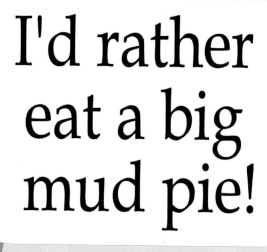

I'd rather
eat a big
mud pie!

My mom stood up,
her eyes stayed on mine.
She walked out of the room
and left me behind.

Gave me a bowl of dark brown mud.

Now here is a meal
you are sure to love.
I brought you a
yummy, muddy pie.

I sat there and
watched her
and tried
not to cry.

I don't like broccoli!
Really I don't!
But I can't eat the mud
in the bowl! I just won't!

Would you eat all the broccoli?

Or just eat the mud?

I scooped up some mud but she didn't flinch! I moved the fork closer to my mouth inch by inch!

She did not grab my fork,
she didn't tell me to stop!
So, I stuck out my tongue,
put the mud right on top!

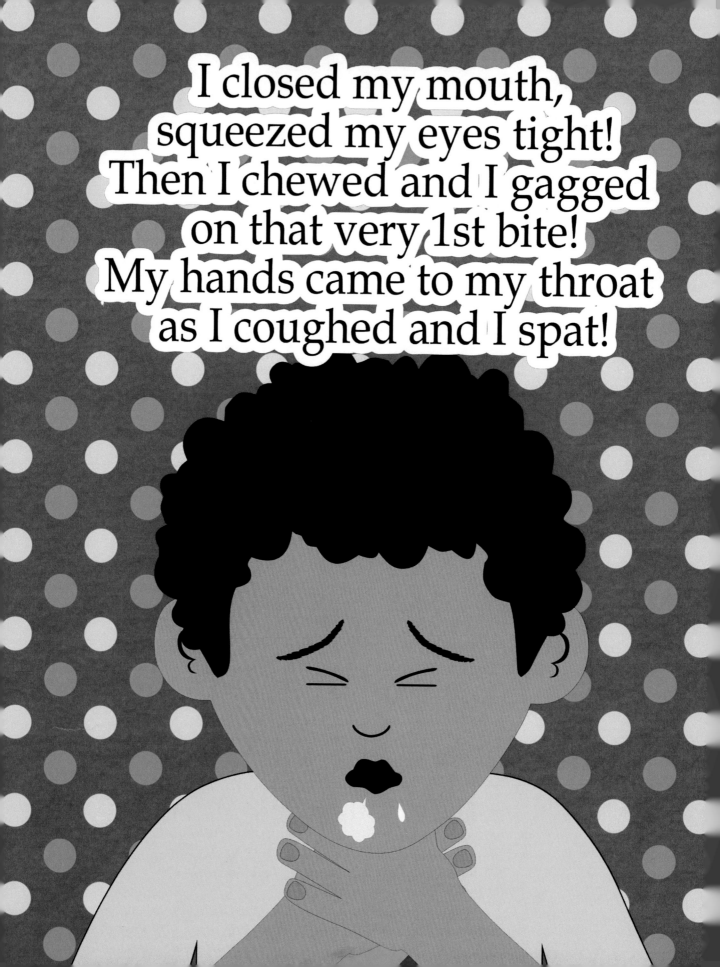

The gooey, dark mud hit the table

Ker-Splat!

WHEW!

Mom put my dinner back in front of me. The mac and cheese

AND

the

broccoli.

I just smiled right back,

You make food that I love

Made in the USA
Lexington, KY
22 April 2019